THE SAND HORSE

Text copyright ©1989 by Ann Turnbull. Illustration copyright ©1989 by Michael Foreman.
This paperback edition first published in 2002 by Andersen Press Ltd. The rights of Ann Turnbull and
Michael Foreman to be identified as the author and illustrator of this work have been asserted by them in accordance
with the Copyright, Designs and Patents Act, 1988. First published in Great Britain in 1989 by Andersen Press Ltd. 20
Vauxhall Bridge Road, London SW1V 2SA. Published in Australia by Random House Australia Pty., 20 Alfred Street,
Milsons Point, Sydney, NSW 2061. Colour separated in Switzerland by Photolitho AG, Zurich.
Printed and bound in Italy by Grafiche AZ, Verona.All rights reserved.
10   9   8   7   6   5   4

British Library Cataloguing in Publication Data available.

ISBN 1 84270 099 5

This book has been printed on acid-free paper

The Sand Horse

Story by Ann Turnbull
Pictures by Michael Foreman

Andersen Press · London

Once there was an artist who lived in St. Ives. He lived with his wife and baby in a house by the sea. Sometimes the artist worked in his studio, but on fine days in summer he went to the beach and made animals in the sand. He could make dogs and cats and seals and dolphins, but mostly he made horses, because horses, he said, were the most beautiful animals of all.

One morning the artist woke to a brisk blue day with a choppy
sea and white crests on the waves.
"Look! White horses!" said his wife.
When the sea is rough and the waves have white tops people
call them white horses.

The artist saw them: far out in the bay, plunging and galloping,
tossing spray from their manes.
"Today I shall make a horse," he said.

He went to the beach. He marked out his pitch, put his hat down on the sand, and started work.

First he fetched water from the sea. He splashed some onto the
dry sand. He patted and moulded the sand.

The horse began to appear: muscles and hooves, raised head and rippling mane.

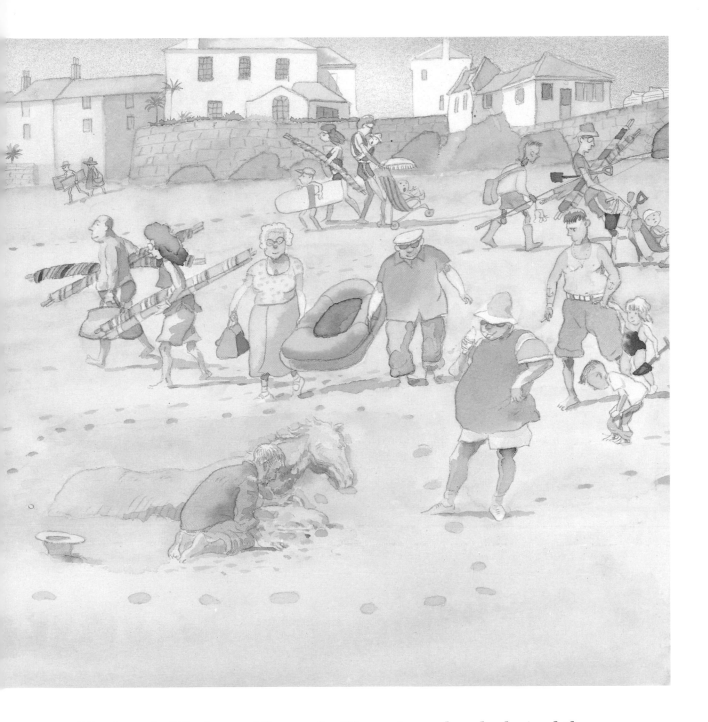

The beach filled up with people. They stopped and admired the
sand horse. They threw money, and the coins chinked in the artist's hat.

The horse grew. He was a galloping horse, galloping forever on his side.

All day the artist worked on his horse, shaping the muscles of his legs and neck, twisting each curl of his mane.

He worked until the sun set and the beach grew cold. Families began leaving. They folded their deck-chairs and shook sand from their clothes.

The artist scooped up the coins in his hat and went home.

The sand horse woke up.
He was alive, but he could not move. He opened his one eye, but all he saw was clouds. He listened with his one ear. He heard seagulls. He heard the boom and hiss of the sea. And faintly, in the crash of waves, he heard neighing.

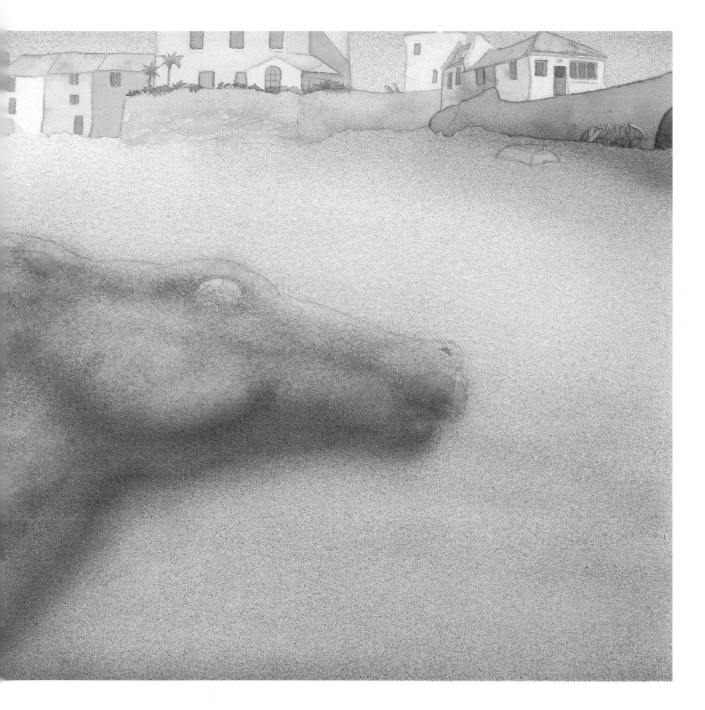

A seagull landed on his back, and walked about, jabbing the air
with his sharp beak.
"Seagull," said the sand horse, "what's that neighing I hear?"
"That's the white horses," said the seagull, "out in the bay."

"What are they doing?"
"They are prancing and frisking and flicking their tails."
"Where are they going?"
"Everywhere!" said the seagull. "Newlyn, Polperro, Mevagissey, Marazion –"

"I want to go with them!" cried the sand horse.
"You!" The seagull wheeled up in the air, laughing, and all his friends joined in. He swooped down again and said, "You! You are only a sand horse. You can't go with them."

The sand horse tried to move. He was a galloping horse, but he was fixed in the sand. He could not go with them.
The sky darkened. The seagulls flew away. The boom of the sea was louder.

Much closer now, the sand horse heard the white horses
neighing.
"Come with us!" they called.
The sea crashed on the shore, flinging spray over the sand horse.

"Come with us!"
The sea crashed again, and the sand horse was soaked with
spray.
"Come with us!" called the white horses. "To Sennen, Land's
End, and the Longships Light!"
A wave broke and flooded the sand horse, drenching his head
and mane.

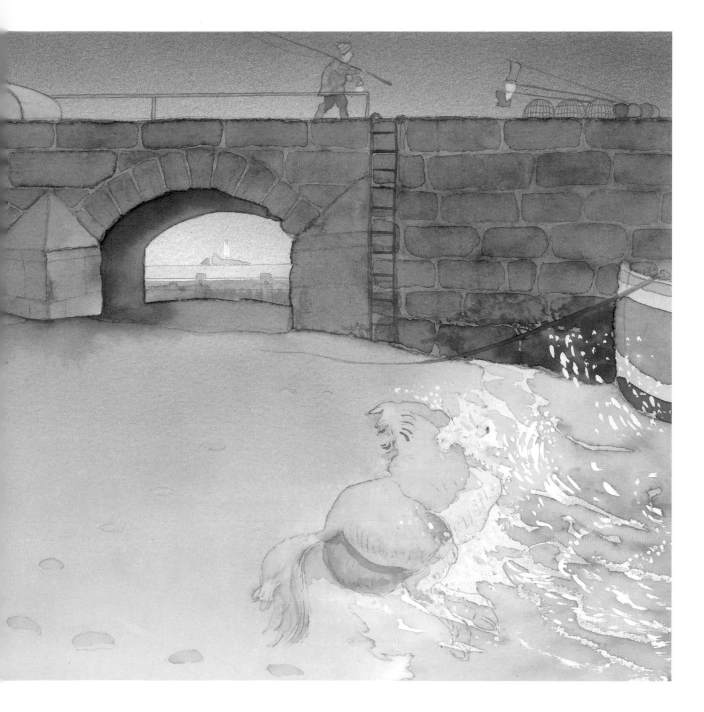

"I'm coming!" he called. "Wait for me!"
Another wave broke, and the sea ran foaming all around the outline of the sand horse, filling every space. The sea sucked and pulled. It was pulling him down the beach.
"I'm coming! I'm coming!" he cried.

A huge wave rolled up the beach. It reared, curled over, and
smashed down upon the sand horse, washing away his mane, his

head, his legs, and his body. It went hissing back down to the sea, dragging the sand horse with it.

The sand horse felt waves buoying him up. Amongst the waves
white horses were prancing. He neighed and tossed his mane.

His hooves struck spray from the sea.
"I can move!" he cried. "I can gallop!"

He frisked and galloped. He swished his white tail.

All around him the white horses plunged and jumped the waves.

"To Sennen!" they neighed. "To Land's End and the Lizard!"

They galloped away, and the sand horse went with them.

Next morning, when the artist came down to the beach, people
looked at the smooth sand and said, "It's a shame. All that work
washed away."
But the artist smiled.
He knew where his sand horse had gone.